*Did the mummy really come alive from time to time?
No one knew for certain — but something was
prowling around!*

British Library Cataloguing in Publication Data
Sibley, Raymond
　　The mummy : from stories by Sir Arthur Conan
　　Doyle.—(Ladybird horror classics. Series 841; 3)
　　I. Title　　II. McBride, Angus　　III. Doyle, *Sir*
　　Arthur Conan
　　823'.914[J]　　PZ7
　　ISBN 0-7214-0883-4

First edition

© LADYBIRD BOOKS LTD MCMLXXXV

*All rights reserved. No part of this publication may be reproduced, stored in a retrieval
system, or transmitted in any form or by any means, electronic, mechanical, photo-
copying, recording or otherwise, without the prior consent of the copyright owner.*

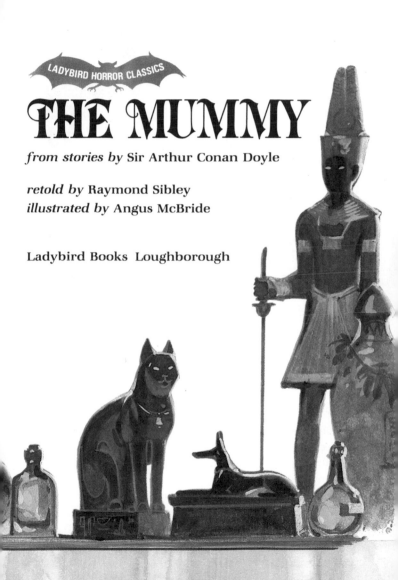

LADYBIRD HORROR CLASSICS

THE MUMMY

from stories by Sir Arthur Conan Doyle

retold by Raymond Sibley
illustrated by Angus McBride

Ladybird Books Loughborough

David Smith stirred uneasily in his bed in the grip of a nightmare. The scene of his dream was a strange underground chamber. How he had got there he did not know, for his legs were heavy and he could not move.

Several stone tables were in the chamber, on each of which lay the form of an Egyptian mummy, covered in rolls of linen. A strange muttering sound began and immediately the bandages on all the mummies started to unwrap themselves, making a crackling noise as one layer peeled off from another.

When the last rolls had curled onto the floor a kind of vapour rose from the bodies, wreathing and swirling like small puffs of smoke.

As these ghost-like wisps piled up Smith saw faces and limbs forming and a high wailing noise came from the half-open mouths.

He covered his eyes but the visions would not be shut out. Grey shapes flitted around him, gently touching his neck with light fingers. Then they changed into figures of terror and with them came a foul and disgusting smell of evil and death.

Smith struggled violently in his dream and finally burst through the bonds of sleep back into his own time, the summer of 1884.

For some moments he shook with fright even though he was relieved to find himself in his own bed in his own room at Old College, Oxford.

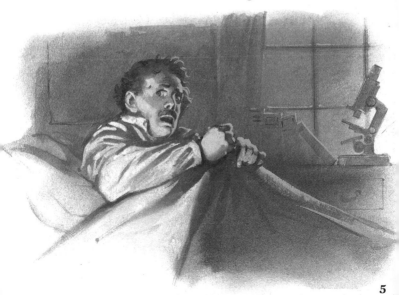

Before he had time to collect himself a long loud scream rang through the building. It was the cry of a man shaken beyond control. Smith got out of bed, his heart pounding.

It must have come from Bellingham in the room beneath, or from Lee on the floor beneath Bellingham. No other students lived in the narrow building, and the sound seemed to be too close to have come from the servants' floor.

There was a rattle of footsteps on the stairs and William Lee burst into the room, half-dressed and white-faced.

'You are a medical student, Smith,' he gasped. 'Please come down! Bellingham's ill.'

Smith followed him down the spiral stone stairs and into Bellingham's sittingroom.

It was more like a museum than a study. The walls and ceiling were covered with relics.

Figures bearing weapons were mixed with almond-eyed Pharaohs and the statues of Egyptian bulls, storks, cats and owls. The gods of Horus, Isis and Osiris peeped down from every shelf. Across the ceiling an open-jawed Nile crocodile hung from a double noose.

Dominating the whole scene was a mummy which lay on a large square table. It was a withered thing with charred head, claw-like hands and bony forearms. Near it was a scroll of yellow parchment. The mummy's case was propped against a wall.

Bellingham sat in an armchair, his head thrown back, his wide-open eyes staring up at the crocodile, his lips blue, his breathing heavy and difficult.

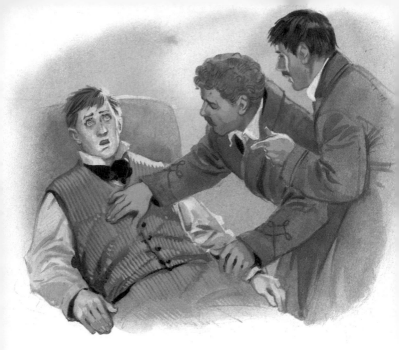

'My God! He's dying,' cried Lee hysterically.

'No. It's just a faint. Give me a hand with him,
Lee. Take his feet. That's right. Now lift him onto
the sofa. If we undo his collar and sprinkle some
water on his face, he'll soon come to. What has he
been doing?'

'I don't know, Smith. He screamed and I ran up
straightaway. I know him quite well. He's engaged
to my sister Eve. It's very good of you to come
down.'

Smith put his hand on Bellingham's chest.

'His heart's beating like a drum. Something has
frightened him. Look at his face! I think we should
throw the rest of the water over him!'

The two students looked at Bellingham closely. His face was white like the underside of a fish. The hair on his head was brown and bristly. His light grey eyes were wide open and stared horribly straight ahead.

'What can have frightened him so?' Smith asked.

'It must be the mummy.'

'The mummy! How?'

'I don't know. This is the second time this has happened. Last winter, before you moved here, he cried out one night. I found him just like this, with that revolting creature in front of him.'

Smith was puzzled.

'Why does he study such things if they frighten him so much?'

'He's a fanatic about the past,' Lee replied. 'He knows more about Ancient Egypt than anyone I know. Ah! I think he's coming to.'

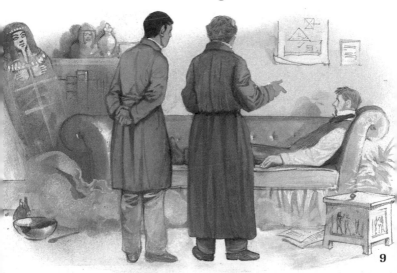

A faint touch of colour had begun to steal back into Bellingham's cheeks and his eyelids quivered. He clasped and unclasped his hands and then drew a long thin breath between his teeth.

Once he realised where he was he sprang from the sofa, seized the roll of parchment, put it in his desk drawer and turned the key.

'What's up?' he asked. 'What are you two doing here?'

'You've been shrieking out and making no end of a fuss,' answered Lee. 'If our neighbour Smith hadn't come down, I don't know what I should have done with you.'

'I'm grateful to you, Smith,' said Bellingham, glancing up at him from his chair.

So saying he sank his head onto his hands and burst into hysterical laughter.

'Look here! Stop that!' cried Smith, shaking him roughly by the shoulder. 'Your nerves are all in a jangle. You must rest and keep quiet for a time and stop this kind of work in the middle of the night, or you'll go off your head. You are all on wires as it is.'

'I wonder,' said Bellingham, 'whether you would be as calm as I am if you had seen...'

'Seen what?'

'Oh, nothing. I meant that I wonder if you could sit up at night in the same room as that mummy without testing your nerves. Maybe you are right. I have been over-working, but I'm all right now. Please don't go for a few minutes.'

'The room is very stuffy,' remarked Lee. 'I'll open the window and let some air in.'

'It's the balsamic resin,' said Bellingham.

He took some leaves from a palm-like plant which was on the table near to the mummy, and held them over the flame of the lamp. A strong biting odour came from the wreaths of smoke.

'It's the sacred plant of the ancient priests,' remarked Bellingham. 'Do you read any Eastern languages, Smith?'

'No. Not a word.'

Bellingham seemed relieved to hear it. Then he continued, 'How long was I unconscious?'

'About four or five minutes.'

'Yes. I thought it could not be very long. Now this mummy was embalmed four thousand years ago. He is in such excellent condition, you would think that he had died only yesterday.'

Smith looked at the mummy with the eye of a medical man. The face, although discoloured, was almost perfect. Two nut-like eyes were sunk into hollow sockets. The skin was very tight over the cheek bones and coarse black hair fell over the ears. Rat-like teeth touched the lower lip.

What Smith did not like was the suggestion of energy about the thing with its bent joints and craned head. The ribs had a parchment-like covering and on the lower body was a long slit where the embalmer had made his mark centuries before.

Coarse yellow bandages covered the legs. Small pieces of myrrh and of cassia had been sprinkled over the whole body.

'He is six feet seven inches tall,' said Bellingham, running his hand over the shrivelled head. 'I don't know his name, so I call him Lot No. 249 because that was his number in the auction sale when I bought him.'

Lee looked at the creature with disgust and shivered slightly. Bellingham also was affected, for his lower lip still trembled, his hands shook and he seemed unable to take his eyes from the mummy.

'You're not going yet,' he cried, as Smith rose from his chair.

'Yes, I must,' replied Smith. 'You are all right now. If I were you, I should take up a study that puts less strain on the nervous system.'

'I'm not usually like this. I've unwrapped bodies before.'

'You fainted last time,' said Lee.

'Yes, so I did. Well, I must take a nerve tonic or something. I think I'll sleep on the sofa in your room, Lee, if you don't mind. Just for tonight.'

Bellingham turned to Smith and shook his hand. 'Goodnight, Smith. I am so sorry to have disturbed you with my foolishness.'

*   *   *

In this strange manner began an acquaintance between Bellingham and Smith. The solid and dependable Smith seemed to have impressed the excitable Bellingham, for he visited the medical student frequently to lend him books, magazines, papers and to talk long hours about Ancient Egypt.

Smith formed the view that Bellingham had a brilliant mind but that despite his cleverness there was a streak of insanity in him.

He noticed also that Bellingham had developed the habit of mumbling and muttering to himself, late at night. It disturbed Smith and distracted him from his work, so he spoke to Bellingham about it. At this the Egyptologist became very angry and denied it.

If Smith had had any doubts about his own hearing he was not long in finding confirmation. Tom Styles, the old servant who looked after the three students, said to him one morning, as he tidied up Smith's rooms, 'If you please, sir, do you think that Mr Bellingham is all right?'

'All right, Styles?'

'I mean right in his head, sir?'

'Of course. Why shouldn't he be?'

'Well, he's not the man he used to be. He's took to talking to himself something awful. I wonder it don't disturb you, being just above him. What to make of him I don't know, sir.'

'It's none of your business, Styles.'

'Maybe not, sir. But I do wonder about the noises I hear coming from his room sometimes, when he's out and the door's locked on the outside.'

'You're talking nonsense, Styles.'

'I've heard them more than once, with my own ears.'

'Rubbish!'

'Very good, sir. You'll ring the bell if you want me.'

Smith thought no more of it during the day, but late that night the words of Styles were brought back to his memory.

Bellingham had called in to see him and was talking about the rock tombs in Upper Egypt, when Smith, whose hearing was remarkably good, distinctly heard the sound of a door opening on the landing below.

'Somebody has just gone into or come out of your room.'

Bellingham sprang to his feet.

'I'm sure I locked the door,' he stammered.

'Maybe you did, but someone is coming up the stairs to us now.'

Bellingham rushed out. Half-way down the stairs Smith heard him stop. There was a sound of whispering. A moment later the door beneath him closed and a key creaked in the lock. Bellingham returned to Smith's room. His face had turned pale and there were beads of moisture on his forehead.

'It's all right,' he said. 'It was my dog. He pushed the door open.'

'I didn't know you had a dog,' remarked Smith, looking thoughtfully at Bellingham's strained face.

'Yes. He's a nuisance. I should remember to lock the door.'

'Why? I should have thought shutting the door would have been enough, without locking it.'

'Well, Styles might let him out by mistake. He's valuable. I don't want to lose him.'

Smith looked hard at Bellingham. 'I know a bit about dogs. May I look at him?'

'Certainly. But not tonight, I have an appointment. Oh dear, I'm late already. Please excuse me!'

So saying, he left. Smith heard him go into his rooms and lock the door on the inside. He did not go out to an appointment.

Smith knew his neighbour had lied twice, for the step on the stairs was not the step of an animal. Then what could it be?

He settled down to work but was soon interrupted again. This time it was his close friend Hastie, another student.

'Still working, Smith! Do you know, if an earthquake came and destroyed Oxford, you would sit calmly in the ruins reading your books.'

'What's the news then?'

'Nothing very much.' Hastie rambled on for some time about cricket, rowing and athletics before another thought struck him.

'By the way, Smith, have you heard about Norton?'

'No.'

'He's been attacked, about a hundred yards from the college gates.'

'Who...'

'If you said "what" you might be nearer the truth. Norton says he doesn't know what it was, and he has some strange scratch marks on his throat.'

'What then?'

'Don't know. Norton says he passes that spot at about the same time every night. A big elm tree from Rainy's garden hangs over the path and something dropped on him out of that. It had him by the throat. Fortunately someone came along the path and it ran away. Norton never got a look at it.'

'A thief, most likely,' said Smith.

'Possibly. I say, your delightful neighbour Bellingham will be pleased when he hears about it. He and Norton hate each other. They had a violent row last winter. From what I know of him, Bellingham is not the man to forget his little debts.'

When Hastie had gone, Smith could not settle down to work. The strange events of the day and the attack on Norton filled his mind.

'Confound Bellingham,' cried Smith, as he threw his book down. 'He has ruined my night's reading and that's reason enough to keep clear of him in future.'

For ten days Smith studied hard. Whenever Bellingham knocked on his door he kept quiet, pretending to be out.

One afternoon, however, as he walked down the spiral stairs, Bellingham's door was flung open and Lee came out, his face alive with anger. Close behind him followed Bellingham, quivering with emotion.

'You'll be sorry for this, Lee,' he hissed.

'Very likely, but the engagement is off! Eve will do as I say. I'd rather she was in her grave than marry you. We don't want to see you again.'

'You promised not to tell.'

'Don't worry. I'll keep my promise. My lips are sealed.'

Smith heard no more, for he hurried down the stairs before he could become involved in their quarrel. It was clearly serious, for Lee to persuade his sister not to see Bellingham again. Smith wondered what could have caused such a breach, and what it was Lee had promised to keep silent about.

Soon he reached the river and spent the whole afternoon watching the races. Hastie, a superb oarsman, won the final of the sculls by a clear length. As Smith prepared to return to his rooms, he felt a touch on his shoulder. It was Lee.

'I want to speak to you about something important, Smith. I've left my college rooms and moved into that cottage over there by the river.

If I were you I should get away from Bellingham and live somewhere else.'

'Why?'

'I can't give a reason,' replied Lee, 'as I have made a promise to be silent. All I will say is that Bellingham is not a safe man to live near.'

'What do you mean?'

'I can't say. We had a violent row today. You must have noticed when you were passing.'

'I guessed something was wrong.'

'Since that night he fainted I've had doubts about him and today he told me things that frightened me. Thank God I found out before he married Eve!'

'I'm sorry Lee, but unless you give me good reason I've no intention of moving from where I'm very comfortable. I'm not afraid of Bellingham or any other man.'

'Very well. I can only warn you.'

With that they parted and Smith returned to his lodgings.

About eight o'clock that evening he decided to take a walk. On his way out he noticed a book that Bellingham had lent him. He felt guilty that he had not returned it, so he picked it up and walked downstairs. There was no answer when he tapped on Bellingham's door, which was unlocked. Pleased to have avoided a meeting, Smith stepped into the room and placed the book upon the table.

The lamp was turned low, but the details of the room were clear. It was all much as he had seen it before, the animal-headed gods, the hanging crocodile and the table littered with scrolls and dried plant leaves. The mummy case stood upright against the wall, but the mummy itself was missing.

Smith felt that he had done Bellingham an injustice, for if he had something to hide he would hardly have left his door unlocked for anyone to enter.

It was pitch black on the spiral staircase. Smith was slowly making his way down its irregular steps when he became aware that something had passed by him in the darkness. There was a faint sound, a whiff of air, and a light brushing of his elbow, but so slight that he could scarcely be certain of it.

He stopped and listened. The wind was rustling among the ivy outside, but he could hear nothing else.

'Is that you, Styles?' he shouted.

There was no answer. Smith continued down the stairs.

He had reached the ground, still turning the matter over in his head, when someone came running swiftly towards him over the lawn.

'Is that you, Smith?'

'Hello, Hastie!'

'For God's sake, come at once. Young Lee has been fished out of the river more dead than alive. The doctor's out. You're the next best qualified. I'll come with you. Harrington is with him.'

'Have you any brandy?'

'No.'

'I'll fetch my flask.'

Smith rushed up the stairs, seized the brandy flask and was hurrying down with it when he noticed something which stopped him in his tracks.

He had closed Bellingham's door. Now it was
open wide. When he had left the room the mummy
case had been empty. Now it was not. In it stood
the grim, stark body of the mummy, its face
towards the door. It appeared to be without life,
but as Smith stared, there lingered a spark of
energy and a faint sign of consciousness in the
sunken eyes.

The voice of Hastie from the bottom of the stairs
brought Smith back to his senses.

'Hurry up, Smith,' he shouted. 'We shall have to
do a sprint.'

Neck and neck they dashed through the falling
darkness, until they reached the cottage.

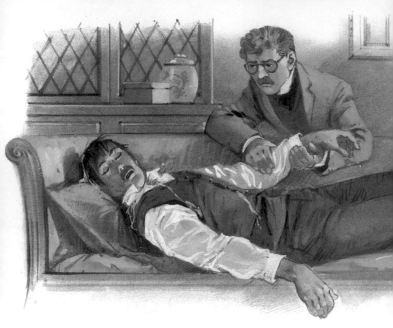

Lee was stretched on the sofa, dripping wet, with green river scum in his hair and a fringe of white foam on his lips. His friend Harrington was trying to rub some warmth back into his rigid limbs.

Smith put his watch glass to Lee's lips. 'Yes,' he said, 'there's dimming on it. He's still alive. You take one arm, Hastie. Now work it as I do, and we'll soon pull him round.'

For ten minutes they worked in silence, inflating and depressing the chest of the unconscious man. At the end of that time a shiver ran through Lee's body, his lips trembled and he opened his eyes. The other three students burst into a cheer.

'Wake up, old chap,' said Harrington. 'You've frightened us enough.'

'Give him some brandy first, and then let him tell us what happened,' said Hastie.

'We were both reading in here,' explained Harrington. 'After a while he went out for a stroll. Shortly afterwards I heard a scream and a splash. By the time I'd pulled him out, all life seemed to have gone. The doctor was out and I had to get help. Luckily I bumped into you, Hastie, or I don't know what I would have done.'

Lee raised himself on his hands. 'What happened?' he asked. 'Ah, yes; I remember now. The water.' A look of fear came into his eyes.

'How did you fall in?'

'I didn't fall in.'

'But Harrington found you in the river.'

After some moments Lee said slowly, 'I was thrown in. Something picked me up from behind as I was standing on the river bank and hurled me in. I heard nothing and I saw nothing, but I know what it was.'

'So do I!' whispered Smith.

Lee looked at him in surprise. 'You've learned then?' he said. 'Well, if you remember, I did warn you.'

'Yes, you did, and I think now I shall take that advice.'

'What the devil are you two on about?' growled Hastie. 'I should think it would be more sensible to get Lee to bed instead of chatting. You can do that when he feels stronger.'

On the way back to college, Smith was silent as he ran through his mind the incidents of the evening. The absence of the mummy from its case; the something that passed him on the stair; the reappearance of the mummy in its case; and the attack on Lee, so similar to the outrage on Norton. Both were men against whom Bellingham had a grudge.

Smith did not speak to Hastie about his suspicions. Hastie would have said that Smith's eyes had deceived him and the mummy had been there all the time. He would have said that Lee had fallen into the river by accident, and the noise on the stair had been a gust of wind. Had the positions been reversed, Smith knew he would have said much the same to Hastie.

Yet he knew that Bellingham was an evil man with murder in his heart. And he was using a weapon such as no one had used before.

As they parted, Hastie said roughly, 'You *are* friendly tonight and no mistake! Hardly a word spoken since we left Lee. Goodnight to you!'

Smith crossed the lawn and then made his way up the stairs. As he reached the first landing, Bellingham's door opened.

'Good evening,' he said politely. 'Won't you come in?'

'No,' replied Smith angrily.

'Oh! Still as busy as ever studying? I wanted to ask you about young Lee. I've heard he's had an accident.' Although his face was serious his tone was mocking.

'Yes,' snapped Smith, 'but you'll be sorry to hear he is out of danger. Your plan didn't work this time. I know all about you, now!'

Bellingham took a step back and half-closed his door. 'What do you mean? I had nothing to do with it.'

'I mean that you and that bag of bones behind you worked it out between you. I'm telling you, Bellingham, if anyone connected with you meets his death, I'll have you up for it. And if they don't hang you, it won't be my fault!'

'You're mad,' retorted Bellingham coolly. With that he slammed his door, and Smith went into his own room in a bad temper.

He sat reading for some time to calm himself. At last he undressed, got into bed, turned out the lamp, and fell asleep.

After an hour or so he was awakened by a sound. He raised himself on his elbows. A clock ticked in the corner. A dog barked in the distance. A cab rattled by in a nearby street.

Out of the darkness he heard steady breathing. Something was in the room with him! It was making its way along the line of the wall towards his bed.

Smith couldn't move. His feet were like ice, his hands tingled and a cold sweat oozed from his face and back.

Two eyes glimmered at him in the dark. The silence was intense. Smith knew he was alone with a thing from a dead civilisation.

Its head was close. He could see straight into its eyes. Claw-like fingers scratched the bedpost as it felt for Smith's face. The stale breath from the thing turned Smith's stomach. It crouched – ready to spring.

Smith sensed that the next moments were going to decide his fate. His fingers seemed locked, his muscles cramped, and his strength gone, but he gathered his courage and screamed out in terror.

Almost immediately there was a loud crash and then the heavy door of his room shut to, with a noise which shook the old building in its fury.

With trembling fingers, Smith lit his lamp.

The scream must have been heard on the servants' floor, for Styles rushed up the stairs and ran panting into Smith's room.

'Did you see anything on the stairs, Styles?' asked the student in a weak voice.

'No, sir! I heard you shout, saw your lamp and I came up straightaway,' gasped Styles.

'Did you hear anything on the stairs, then?'

'No, sir.'

'Something came into my bedroom to attack me.'

'I'll go and check with Mr Bellingham.'

As he waited, recovering his strength, Smith heard the knocks on Bellingham's door and later, the returning footsteps of Styles.

'I can hear noises in there but I can't wake him. If I were you I should go back to bed, Mr Smith, and get some rest. You have had a bad dream. That's all.'

Smith locked and bolted the door, but he did not go back to sleep. He sat in an armchair, staring at the window, waiting for the dawn.

Next morning, Smith saw nothing of Bellingham. Harrington came however to say that Lee was making good progress, and had almost recovered.

All day Smith kept to his books but as evening approached he felt that a walk in the country, to visit his friend Dr Peterson, would do him more good than the strained atmosphere of his lodgings.

Smith stepped out briskly, breathing the fresh country air into his lungs. The college was on the edge of town and soon he was tramping the lonely lane that led to Dr Peterson's house. The moonlight turned the hedges and trees to silver. No one else was about.

He reached the iron gate which opened into the long gravel drive up to the house. The cosy light from its windows glimmered through the trees. As Smith put his hand on the iron latch of the gate, he glanced back along the road.

Something was coming swiftly down it.

The thing moved in the shadow of the hedge. As it closed on him Smith saw a thin neck and two eyes that would ever haunt his dreams.

With a cry of terror he turned and ran for his life up the gravel drive.

He heard the gate open and clang to, then a swift patter of feet behind him. Wildly he rushed through the night. As he looked back in terror over his shoulder, he saw the horror racing up to him with blazing eyes and bony arm outstretched. Nearer it came, making a hoarse, gurgling noise in its throat.

Smith flung himself at the door, opened it, bolted it behind him and fell in a half-faint on the hall floor.

'What on earth is the matter, Smith?' exclaimed the doctor from the door of his study.

'Please, some brandy first.'

'Are you all right?' said the doctor, as Smith drank the brandy at one gulp. 'You are as white as a ghost.'

'May I sleep here tonight, Peterson? I dare not face that road again in the dark!'

'Of course. Now, come into my study and tell me what is the matter.'

Smith did so. He told of the events in their order, from the night that Lee had called him to attend Bellingham, up to the last attempt on his own life.

When Smith had finished, Dr Peterson sat silent for some time puffing at his pipe. At last he said, 'I never heard of such a thing in my life, never! If they are the true facts of the matter, I should like to hear what you make of them.'

'I think,' said Smith quietly, 'that Bellingham found out from his Eastern studies how to bring a mummy – or possibly only this mummy – to life, if only for a short time. Then the idea came to him to use it for his own ends.'

'You mean the attacks on Norton, Lee and yourself?'

'Yes. All the people against whom he had a grudge. It is only by chance he has not three murders on his conscience.'

'Come, Smith old chap, you are taking it all too seriously. Your nerves are frayed from over-study. Tonight you came here with your head full of Bellingham. Some tramp creeps after you, sees you run in fright and chases you to rob you. Your imagination did the rest.'

'No, no! It is not fancy.'

'I admit you have cause for strong suspicions against Bellingham, but you have no hard evidence. If you take this to the police they will laugh at you.'

'I know,' replied the student in grim fashion. 'That's why I mean to take care of the matter myself. I must do it for my own safety.'

'Do what?'

'First I am going to write down a full statement of all that I have told you. Then I would like you to sign it as a witness and date it. The date is very important.'

'Why?'

'Because I may be arrested for what I am going to do and you will have to produce this statement as evidence in my favour.'

*   *   *

The next morning Smith walked slowly back to Oxford. Just after nine he stopped at Cliffords, the gunsmiths in the High Street and bought a revolver and a box of cartridges. He loaded six of them into the revolver, half-cocked the weapon, and placed it carefully in his overcoat pocket. Then he made his way to Hastie's rooms.

'Hastie, I want you to do what I ask without asking any questions.'

'All right.'

'Bring a heavy walking stick with you and lend me your longest amputating knife.'

'I say, you are on the warpath this morning!'

Smith put the amputating knife in his coat and led Hastie across the lawn towards Bellingham's rooms.

'I think I can do this alone, Hastie,' said Smith grimly. 'If I have only Bellingham to deal with I shan't need you, but if I shout then come up the stairs as quickly as you can.'

'All right, I'll wait here.'

'I may be some time, so don't budge until I come down again.'

Smith ascended the stairs, pushed open Bellingham's door and stepped inside. Bellingham was seated at his table, writing.

Very deliberately Smith crossed the room to the fireplace, struck a match and lit the fire. Bellingham watched him with amazement and rage on his face.

'Just make yourself at home, Smith! Don't mind me!' he gasped.

Smith did not reply. He sat down and put his watch on the table, took out his pistol, cocked it, and placed it near to the watch. Then he threw down the long amputating knife in front of Bellingham and said, 'Now get to work and cut up that mummy.'

'Oh, that's it, is it?' sneered Bellingham.

'Yes, it is. They tell me that the law can't touch you, but I have a law of my own. I give you one minute. If you haven't started by then I'll put a bullet through your head.'

Bellingham's face turned the colour of putty. 'You would murder me?'

'Yes.'

'For what?'

'To stop your evil.'

'But what have I done?'

'You know very well.'

'You are mad, Smith! Why should I destroy my own property? It is a very valuable mummy.'

'You must cut it up and burn it.'

'I will not!'

Smith took up the pistol and raised it towards Bellingham. The seconds ticked by. Smith put his finger on the trigger. His face was expressionless.

'All right! I'll do it!' screamed Bellingham. He snatched up the knife and hacked at the figure of the mummy. The creature crackled and snapped under every stab of the blade. A thick yellow dust rose from it. Spices and dried essences rained down on the floor. Suddenly, with a loud crack, the mummy's backbone snapped and it became a heap of sprawling limbs on the floor.

'Now into the fire!' said Smith. The flames leaped and roared as the dried pieces were piled on the fire. Soon the room was like the stoke-hole of a steamer. Sweat streamed down the faces of the two men, but still Bellingham stooped and worked while Smith watched him with a set face.

A thick smoke came from the fire and the air was so heavy with the smell of burned hair and bone, that it was difficult to breathe.

After about a quarter of an hour, Bellingham, with hate and fear in his eyes, turned to Smith, and snarled, 'Perhaps that will satisfy you?'

'No; I'm going to make a clean sweep of all your things. Put those leaves and plants on the fire, they may have something to do with it.'

'What now?' asked Bellingham, after they had been added to the blaze.

'The roll of parchment with the writing on it. You had it the night you fainted. It's in that locked drawer, I think.'

'No, no,' shouted Bellingham. 'Not that! Please don't burn that! You don't know what you are doing.'

'Open the drawer!'

'Please Smith! I'll teach you what is in it. I'll translate it for you. I'll share it with you. All right then, but let me make a copy before you burn it.'

Smith stood up, turned the key in the drawer, took out the yellow curled roll of parchment and threw it into the fire.

Bellingham screamed and put his hand into the fire, but Smith gripped him by the collar, at the same time pressing the parchment into the flames with his heel until it had caught light.

'Now, Master Bellingham,' said Smith, releasing him, 'I think I've stopped your little games. If I were you I should leave this college, for if I suspect you have returned to your old tricks, I shall pay you another visit. Now I'm going back to my studies.'

The door closed behind him, leaving Bellingham quite alone. He turned his head in the direction of the fire.

A few charred and brittle sticks were all that remained of Lot No. 249.

Stories . . .
that have stood the test of time

SERIES 740
LADYBIRD CHILDREN'S CLASSICS

Gulliver's Travels

Treasure Island

Swiss Family Robinson

Secret Garden

A Journey to the Centre of the Earth

The Three Musketeers

A Tale of Two Cities

The Lost World

King Solomon's Mines

Hound of the Baskervilles

Around the World in Eighty Days

A Christmas Carol

The Wind in the Willows

The Last of the Mohicans

The Happy Prince and other stories

Peter Pan

Lorna Doone

Oliver Twist

The Railway Children

Kidnapped

A Little Princess

SERIES 740
FABLES AND LEGENDS

Aladdin & his wonderful lamp

Ali Baba & the forty thieves

Famous Legends (Book 1)

Famous Legends (Book 2)

Aesop's Fables (Book 1)

Aesop's Fables (Book 2)

La Fontaine's Fables: The Fox turned Wolf

Folk Tales from around the World

Robin Hood

SERIES SL – LARGE FORMAT

Aesop's Fables

Gulliver's Travels

SERIES 841
HORROR CLASSICS

Dracula

Frankenstein

The Mummy

Ladybird titles cover a wide range of subjects and reading ages.
Write for a free illustrated list from the publishers:
LADYBIRD BOOKS LTD Loughborough Leicestershire England
and USA – LADYBIRD BOOKS INC Lewiston Maine 04240